US MILITARY CAREERS

US SPECIAL OPERATIONS FORCES

BY MARCIA AMIDON LUSTED

CONTENT CONSULTANT
Michael W. Howland, M.C.J.
Master Sergeant, US Army (Retired)
Adjunct Professor of Legal Studies
University of Mississippi

An Imprint of Abdo Publishing | abdobooks.com

ABDOBOOKS.COM

Published by Abdo Publishing, a division of ABDO, PO Box 398166, Minneapolis, Minnesota 55439. Copyright © 2021 by Abdo Consulting Group, Inc. International copyrights reserved in all countries. No part of this book may be reproduced in any form without written permission from the publisher. Essential Library™ is a trademark and logo of Abdo Publishing.

Printed in the United States of America, North Mankato, Minnesota.
042020
092020

THIS BOOK CONTAINS RECYCLED MATERIALS

Cover Photo: K. Kassens/US Army/Defense Visual Information Distribution Service
Interior Photos: Fred W. Baker III/US Army, 4–5; Cpl. William Chockey/US Marine Corps/Defense Visual Information Distribution Service, 7, 28–29, 50–51, 55; Staff Sgt. Justin Moeller/US Army/Defense Visual Information Distribution Service, 11, 90–91; Patrick A. Albright/Maneuver Center of Excellence and Fort Benning Public Affairs/US Army/Defense Visual Information Distribution Service, 14–15; Pfc. William Gore/US Army/Defense Visual Information Distribution Service, 17; Senior Chief Mass Communication Specialist Jayme Pastoric/US Navy, 21; Tech. Sgt. Rebeccah Woodrow/US Air Force/Defense Visual Information Distribution Service, 26; AP Images, 33; Susan Walsh/AP Images, 37; Mass Communication Specialist 2nd Class Shauntae Hinkle-Lymas/US Navy, 38; Mass Communication Specialist 2nd Class Russell Rhodes Jr./US Navy, 40–41; US Navy, 44, 96; Senior Chief Mass Communication Specialist Jayme Pastoric/US Navy/Defense Visual Information Distribution Service, 47; Staff Sgt. Iman Broady-Chin/US Army/Defense Visual Information Distribution Service, 58, 67; Joe Ernst/Fort McCoy, Wis./US Army/Defense Visual Information Distribution Service, 62–63; US Navy Photo/Alamy, 70–71; Cpl. Heather J. Atherton/US Marine Corps/Defense Visual Information Distribution Service, 74; Airman 1st Class Taryn Butler/US Air Force/Defense Visual Information Distribution Service, 78–79; Airman 1st Class Nathaniel Hudson/US Air Force/Defense Visual Information Distribution Service, 83; EJ Hersom/Department of Defense/Defense Visual Information Distribution Service, 84; Kevin Maurer/AP Images, 93

Editor: Charly Haley
Series Designer: Nikki Nordby

LIBRARY OF CONGRESS CONTROL NUMBER: 2019954350

PUBLISHER'S CATALOGING-IN-PUBLICATION DATA

Names: Lusted, Marcia Amidon, author.
Title: US Special Operations Forces / by Marcia Amidon Lusted
Description: Minneapolis, Minnesota : Abdo Publishing, 2021 | Series: US military careers | Includes online resources and index.
Identifiers: ISBN 9781532192319 (lib. bdg.) | ISBN 9781098210212 (ebook)
Subjects: LCSH: Special force troops--Juvenile literature. | Special forces (Military science)--United States--Juvenile literature. | Military power--Juvenile literature. | Armed Forces--Juvenile literature.
Classification: DDC 355.12--dc23

CONTENTS

CHAPTER ONE
On the Job

CHAPTER TWO
A Proud Tradition

CHAPTER THREE
Special Forces Command

CHAPTER FOUR
Navy SEALs

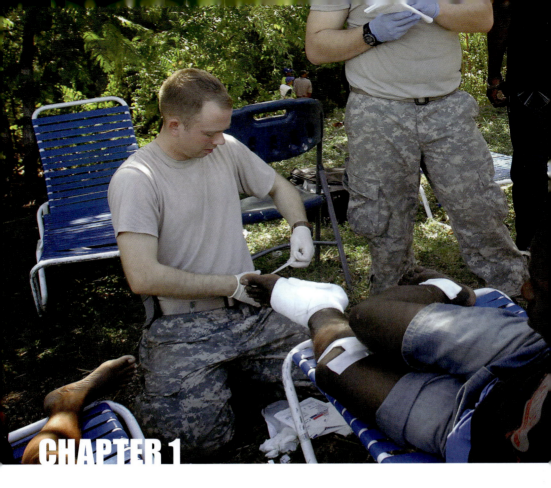

CHAPTER 1

ON THE JOB

The line of villagers stretched far down the road. US Army Special Forces medics had put the word out that they would help sick and injured people in a tiny village in Bolivia. They expected about 500 local people to show up. But on the day of the free clinic, nearly 10,000 villagers came.

A special operations medical sergeant in the US Army Special Forces, also called the Green Berets, was helping with the

The US Army sets up medical clinics all over the world.

free clinic. He and his unit were engaged in counternarcotics operations in the countries along the Andes mountain range. They were working with other US agencies to stop the illegal drug trade. Many villagers grew coca plants, used to make cocaine. It was not illegal to grow these plants in Bolivia because they were used for legal products such as tea and medicine. So the villagers were angry. They thought the US soldiers were trying to take away their farms and starve them. Sometimes the villagers blocked roads around the US Army base or threw small explosives.

The special operations medical sergeant was trained to provide emergency medical care for the army unit. He could also provide routine and long-term medical care. He and the other medics set up field hospitals to treat any army personnel injured in battle or other activities. They were certified medical paramedics and knew how to care for traumatic injuries. They were also trained in veterinary medicine.

But another part of the sergeant's job as a medic was to build trust with the people who lived in the area. The villagers were already angry at the army soldiers. So, the sergeant and the other medics would tell the villagers that they were having a sick call. This meant the army clinic would treat anyone, including civilians, for a certain amount of time. Thousands of people came with their sick children. Adults who had been hurt while logging or doing other jobs also came. The medics helped teach people about diseases and how to stay healthy. Army dentists helped people with tooth problems. The medics even helped injured animals such as cows and goats. In just one day, a medic treated several people. He helped a woman with a severe toothache who had never seen a dentist before. He bandaged the arm of a child who had been cut by a rock. He even treated a sore on the leg of a family's goat by putting ointment on it. Another medic delivered the baby of a pregnant woman who had walked for miles over mountain paths to receive medical care.

★ US Army Special Forces soldiers are among the most highly trained in the military.

The sergeant's career in the US Army Special Forces Green Berets may seem straightforward. He is an army medic, and his job is to treat wounded soldiers on the battlefield. However, his job is much more. He is often a goodwill ambassador in countries where the people are suspicious of foreigners. He carries a weapon and has been trained in combat. But his real tools are his medical knowledge and his ability to make people feel better, both physically and mentally.

MORE THAN FIGHTING

When people think about the armed forces, and especially the Special Operations Forces groups from each branch of the military, they tend to think it is all about fighting. Special Operations Forces members have a reputation. It often comes from Hollywood movies, which show them as being extremely good fighters who sneak into foreign countries and carry out difficult and dangerous missions. And while this is often true, those kinds of missions could not happen without the people

WOMEN IN THE SPECIAL OPERATIONS FORCES

Mostly because of Hollywood's portrayal of Special Operations Forces units as being made up only of men, many people think that women aren't a part of the Special Operations Forces and never have been. Both of those assumptions are wrong. Women have been involved in special operations since World War II (1939–1945). Today, they are part of all Special Operations Forces units. They are commanders, analysts, pilots, and coordinators of civilian and military interactions. They also serve on the front lines in intelligence and combat operations. This became possible when women were allowed to serve in combat roles in 2013. In 2016, women were permitted to serve in combat in any branch of the military, including in Special Operations Forces units.

who do many other jobs within those same Special Operations Forces groups. Serving in the Special Operations Forces isn't just about combat. It's also about working with local people in foreign countries to make sure they are safe, especially if they live in an area of conflict or illegal activity. It's about teaming up with the armed forces of other countries to provide training and helping them when they need military aid to defend themselves. Special Operations Forces design and build new roads and bridges. They also help people all over the world during natural disasters or other catastrophes.

   The main job of the Special Operations Forces members and support staff is to carry out unconventional operations during both peace and wartime. Unconventional operations may involve helping a resistance movement in another country. These movements might include disrupting or overthrowing a government or a ruling power. Special Operations Forces work with underground or guerrilla organizations in that country. These are small groups that are not part of a country's regular army, and they do not support the country's government. Underground and guerrilla groups often fight in unusual ways. The help that Special Operations Forces units give them might include reconnaissance of enemy forces. Special Operations Forces may also help a group to conduct raids or demolitions of enemy strongholds.

The work of Special Operations Forces may also involve search-and-rescue missions for hostages or other military personnel. It might involve carrying out operations for counterterrorism or antidrug activities. Special Operations Forces may work by air, on land, or by sea.

THE BEST OF THE BEST

All Special Operations Forces members have first enlisted in a branch of the US military. The army, the navy, the marines,

WHY JOIN SPECIAL OPERATIONS FORCES?

Air Force Master Sergeant Jose Cervantes, a pararescueman who is part of one of the Special Tactics teams in the US Air Force, talked about his reason for joining the Air Force Special Ops Pararescue unit. Pararescuemen are medically trained members of the air force who parachute to rescue people in remote areas:

> When I was a sophomore in high school, I watched about a 40-minute special on pararescue. And, you know, interesting things, like, the fact that there was only several hundred of them, where the Navy SEALs, there's several thousand of them. And so the next day, I went to the Air Force recruiting office, and I asked, "What are the steps that I have to take to get in the Air Force and pursue this pararescue thing?" My [Air Force] class ended up graduating seven out of 96 candidates, and I was one of them. . . . I knew that I'd chosen something special, something that was going to make a direct impact on our nation. And I knew I was going to help people on a daily basis.[1]

★ Army Special Forces soldiers climb into a US Navy helicopter. Different Special Operations Forces units sometimes work or train together.

and the air force all have their own Special Operations Forces groups. The army has the Green Berets, the Night Stalkers, and the Rangers. The navy has the Sea, Air, and Land (SEAL) Teams and the Special Warfare Combatant-Craft Crewmen (SWCC). The marines have the Marine Corps Forces Special Operations Command (MARSOC) and the Marine Corps Force Reconnaissance (Force Recon). The air force has Air Force

Special Ops, which includes Special Tactics Teams. There are also the antiterrorism Special Operations Forces, which are the army's Delta Force and the navy's Special Warfare Development Group (DEVGRU), also known as SEAL Team 6.

Enlisted men and women who wish to become part of any of the Special Operations Forces units have to apply and meet strict standards of fitness and mental ability. Then they go through extensive training. First, they train in general combat. They learn survival skills and military tactics, and they receive weapons training. Then they receive extra training related to their specific Special Operations Forces unit. This could include training in areas such as foreign languages, swimming and diving, medicine, parachuting, and flying aircraft. Many do not

SPECIAL OPERATIONS FORCES TECHNOLOGY

General Joseph Votel previously served as the leader of the US Special Operations Command (SOCOM), which is a command center in charge of organizing, training, and equipping all Special Operations Forces as well as supporting antiterrorism operations for the Department of Defense. He explained how Special Operations Forces soldiers train hard across many different areas and use advanced technology in their operations around the world. "The reality is, a lot of training and rehearsing . . . goes into these operations," Votel said in a TV news interview.[2] The technology used by Special Operations Forces ranges from advanced drones and helicopters to high-tech night-vision devices. Votel also noted that all Special Operations Forces personnel must undergo battlefield medical training.

make it through the training phase and drop out because it is too difficult. Once they are accepted and become part of a Special Operations Forces unit, they may find themselves working anywhere in the world, often in harsh climates and unsafe conditions. Soldiers in the Special Operations Forces are often referred to as "the best of the best" because they must work and train extremely hard to reach that level.

CAREERS

In any Special Operations Forces unit, regardless of which military branch it is in, people find their specialties and choose specific careers within that unit. Often new unit members have firm ideas of what their interests are and what careers they want to pursue. Others go through testing to determine what their strengths are and what careers those strengths are best suited for. Some Special Operations Forces careers are similar to jobs civilians do in the nonmilitary world. Others are very specialized and related only to the types of missions and operations that Special Operations Forces units engage in. Each Special Operations Forces group is different, and each was started for a specific purpose. To understand who they are, what they do, and how they are unique, it is necessary to go back to the origins of their branches of the military, starting with the earliest days of the United States as a country.

CHAPTER 2
A PROUD TRADITION

The US Special Operations Forces belong to different branches of the military, but they share a proud tradition of serving and protecting their country. Some Special Operations Forces units come from military branches that are as old as the United States itself. Others have been created within the last fifty years.

The Army Rangers are among the oldest groups in the US military.

THE ARMY

On June 14, 1775, the Second Continental Congress, which governed the American colonies, formed the Continental army. The army was vital to fighting against British forces as the colonies sought independence. General George Washington was the first commander in chief of the Continental army, which became the US Army. Under his command, the army defeated the British and won independence for the United States as

15

a country. Washington went on to become the first president of the United States.

One of the US Army's most famous Special Operations Forces groups, the Army Rangers, is actually older than the army itself. It was formed in the 1700s when Captain Benjamin Church and Major Robert Rogers each formed a unit to fight in King Philip's War (1675–1676) and the French and Indian War (1754–1763). Rogers wrote the 19 standing orders, which are guidelines for behavior that are still used by the Rangers today. The Rangers served through the American Civil War (1861–1865) and then were inactive until 1941, when the United States became involved in World War II (1939–1945). Six Ranger units were reactivated at that time. They continue to serve today.

Another well-known army Special Operations Forces unit is called the Army Special Forces, nicknamed the Green Berets for their distinctive uniform berets. While earlier versions of this unit existed, the Army Special Forces as it is known today was defined during World War II by the Office of Strategic Services (OSS), a secret intelligence agency that later became the Central Intelligence Agency (CIA). The OSS needed a group of soldiers who could go on secret missions behind the lines of the enemy Axis nations (Germany, Italy, and Japan). The Allied powers (the United States, Great Britain, France, China, and the Soviet Union) fought against the Axis during World War II.

★ The Green Berets held a ceremony in October 2019 to honor President John F. Kennedy's contributions to their unit.

The Green Berets successfully performed many missions to help win the war. Although the OSS disbanded after World War II, Army Brigadier General Robert McClure received permission in 1952 to create a special group of soldiers who would be able to carry out top-secret missions on behalf of the government. The Green Berets began with just ten soldiers but quickly grew.

In 1961, after visiting the Green Beret unit at Fort Bragg, North Carolina, President John F. Kennedy said that the green beret worn by the soldiers was "a symbol of excellence, a badge of courage, a mark of distinction in the fight for freedom."[1] Since then, the Green Berets have carried out thousands of missions, most of them secret.

The army also has an elite special missions unit, which is called the 1st Special Forces Operational Detachment-Delta. It is commonly known as Delta Force. The unit is specifically focused on counterterrorism activities. It was formed in 1977. Most of its missions are classified and not understood outside of the US Army itself. The missions usually involve capturing high-level terrorist leaders or breaking apart terrorist groups. Delta Force often works with the CIA or protects high-ranking government leaders when they visit unstable foreign countries. Although Delta Force has been officially renamed Army Compartmented Elements, it is still best known as Delta Force. This is the name most people associate with the unit, largely because of its use in movies and television shows.

The army also has several airborne regiments that were created specifically to support all Special Operations Forces. An airborne unit is transported by aircraft, and they often parachute into conflicts. One of them is the 160th Special Operations Aviation Regiment, known as the Night Stalkers. Created from the 101st Airborne Division, the Night Stalkers pioneered many night flying techniques and developed special equipment. They were officially recognized as a special unit in 1981, and they carry out missions where there is a need to strike during darkness, undetected by the enemy. Their motto is "Night Stalkers Don't Quit."

THE NAVY

The US Navy is just a few months younger than the army. On October 13, 1775, the Second Continental Congress voted to outfit two sailing vessels with guns and a crew of 80 sailors. Their mission was to intercept any ships carrying ammunition and supplies to the British troops in the American colonies.

IN THE NEWS

Because of their secretive nature, Special Operations Forces missions don't usually make the news. But on May 2, 2011, the US Navy's SEAL Team 6 made the headlines when it captured and killed Osama bin Laden, leader of the terrorist group al-Qaeda. Al-Qaeda is a terrorist group founded by bin Laden that committed the September 11, 2001, terrorist attacks against the United States. Nearly 3,000 people died when terrorists hijacked two airplanes and flew them into the World Trade Center twin towers in New York City.[2] Another hijacked plane crashed into the Pentagon in Washington, DC, killing nearly 200 people. During Operation Neptune Spear, SEAL Team 6 raided an al-Qaeda compound in Abbottabad, Pakistan. In just nine minutes, they found and killed bin Laden in what is now called a nearly perfect mission. A US Navy ship then buried bin Laden's body at sea in an undisclosed location.

The navy was born from this congressional action. Today, as the world's largest navy, the US Navy is known as the most lethal force on the seas. Its forces are capable of preventing aggressive actions by other military forces or by civilians. It is their job to fight piracy, keep the world's seas open for ships to freely cross, and participate in battles at sea.

The navy's Special Operations Forces consist of the Navy SEALs and the SWCC. The SEALs were formed in 1943 from the Naval Construction Battalions (known as the Seabees). While the Seabees still exist as their own unit today, some volunteers from the Seabees were divided into teams, called Navy Combat Demolition Units (NCDUs). Their job was to move ahead of landing groups and check beaches to remove any obstacles. During the Korean War (1950–1953), they began demolishing enemy bridges and tunnels and clearing mines from harbors. In 1962, the NCDUs were formed into SEAL team units. SEAL teams are especially good at starting military strike operations from the water and then returning to the water when they are done, but they also operate on the land and in the air. They carry out missions of unconventional warfare, underwater demolition, and strikes against guerrilla groups.

The SWCC are a companion group of the SEALs. Formed into Special Boat Teams, they are responsible for operating the most modern boats of the navy's fleet. These boats developed

★ Navy SEALs are trained for combat in ocean waters and many other environments.

from the PT boats used in World War II, which were military motorboats designed to carry torpedoes, and the so-called Brown Water Navy of the Vietnam War (1954–1975), which were boats that could travel in the muddy, sediment-filled rivers of Vietnam. The SWCC's mission is to carry out and support the missions of the SEAL teams, delivering teams to their mission sites and getting them out once their missions are completed. The SWCC boat teams can move quickly in shallow water where larger boats cannot go, and they can also drop combat boats by parachute if necessary.

The navy also has a special group formed from SEAL team members. It is commonly known as SEAL Team 6. It is the navy's counterterrorism group, and only the most elite SEAL team members are chosen. Its operations are not limited to water; they also include airborne and land operations. Within DEVGRU are special squadrons for reconnaissance and surveillance. These squadrons collect intelligence before a major DEVGRU strike. There is also a special marine operations squadron, which concentrates on missions that must take place in the water. DEVGRU can also provide security and protection for important people such as political leaders.

THE MARINES

The motto of the US Marine Corps is "Semper Fidelis" or "Always Faithful." The marines are a separate military branch within the Department of the Navy, which is part of the US Department of Defense. The Department of the Navy also holds the US Coast Guard during times of war. The army and the air force have their own separate departments under the Department of Defense.

The marine corps was created on November 10, 1775. The mission of the marines is to provide troops to seize or defend military bases. They also conduct operations in the air or on water as part of navy campaigns. Marines also serve aboard certain naval vessels and provide security at navy bases onshore and at embassies for US diplomats in foreign countries.

They also specialize in amphibious landings, when troops are brought by boat and land on shores during conflicts. The Marine Band is also the oldest military musical group in the United States and performs at special events at the White House.

One of the marines' special forces groups is MARSOC. MARSOC includes a Marine Raider Regiment, which is one of the marines' combat units. They are specially trained in direct fighting, special reconnaissance, helping foreign countries defend themselves when they need help, counterterrorism, and unconventional warfare. The Marine Ranger Support Group provides the communications, logistics, and intelligence for MARSOC.

The marines also have Force Recon. Its main mission is to gather intelligence information for marine operations. It also does reconnaissance by water, swimming or using

OFFICER AND ENLISTED

In every branch of the military, there are officers and there are enlisted personnel. Enlisted members make up about 82 percent of the military.[3] They do most of the specific jobs in the military, from repairing equipment to fighting in combat. Officers are the leaders and managers. They plan missions, give orders, and decide what soldiers are assigned where. There are two ranks of officers: commissioned officers, who have college degrees, and noncommissioned officers, who are enlisted soldiers who have moved up in the ranks during their military careers.

small boats. Force Recon works to prevent piracy at sea and performs searches and seizures on ships that are suspected of illegal activity. Reconnaissance missions are known as green operations. Search and seizure and counterpiracy actions are called black operations. Force Recon marines are trained in parachuting (including special high-altitude techniques), skiing, and amphibious techniques such as working with scuba gear.

THE AIR FORCE

The US Air Force started out as the aeronautical division of the US Army's Signal Corps, which was responsible for communications. In 1907, it consisted of one officer and two enlisted men, and its aircraft consisted of kite balloons used for aerial reconnaissance until the division got its first airplane in 1908. As airplanes developed and became more useful in combat, the Signal Corps' aeronautical division became more important. In 1926, the group became the US Army Air Corps. World War II saw airplanes become even more important in combat as the United States became a global power. In 1947, the division officially became the US Air Force, its own branch of the military.

Today the mission of the US Air Force is "to fly, fight, and win in air, space and cyberspace." The air force's Special Operations Forces, or Air Force Special Ops, has Special Tactics Teams that are highly trained to carry out missions. These missions include air and ground operations. They include assisting strike forces in deploying quickly to any place in the world. A Special Tactics Team is made up of airmen with specific training in certain areas. These specialists include combat controllers, who can perform air traffic control in any place, no matter how rugged. Air traffic control means managing how and when planes take off and land and keeping planes from flying into each other. Combat controllers may have to do this under hostile conditions, such as being under fire from enemy forces. Pararescue experts are medical professionals who can rescue and treat injured personnel on site. Special reconnaissance airmen are experts in surveillance, reconnaissance, and

PART KITE, PART BALLOON

Balloons were used by the US Army as early as the Civil War to try to see battlefields and enemy movements. The aeronautical division of the Army Signal Corps, which would eventually become the Army Air Corps and then the US Air Force, began with the use of kite balloons. These were large, sausage-shaped balloons divided into two cells by an inside diaphragm. The top cell was inflated with hydrogen gas, and the bottom was filled with air for ballast. There were stabilizers and a rudder toward the back of the balloon. Four steel cables held the balloon to the ground. These balloons were used for aerial observation during World War I and World War II, especially at battlefields and front lines of fighting. They did not move across distances; they stayed tethered in one place. In 1905, the army opened a school at Fort Omaha, Nebraska, to teach soldiers how to use these kite balloons.

A member of Air Force Special Ops looks out the window of an HH-60G Pave Hawk helicopter.

electronic warfare. They can precisely target objects or places from very far away and successfully strike them with weapons. They are also skilled at using small unmanned aircraft systems (also called drones), going in and rescuing other military personnel, and using advanced special tactics. Tactical Air Control Party specialists can manage lethal and nonlethal air operations. Special Operations Surgical Teams can perform surgery and other medical procedures anywhere the US military is engaged in missions or operations. As groups, the Special Tactics Teams have been involved in almost every US military conflict since 2001, and they have frequently been involved in direct combat.

As different branches of the US military each have their own Special Operations Forces, there is a great deal of special operations activity happening around the world at any given time. How does the military as a whole coordinate who is doing what, where, and at what time? It has a central command unit for its Special Operations Forces.

CHAPTER 3

SPECIAL FORCES COMMAND

The US military consists of five branches. Between them, there are ten different Special Operations Forces groups. There are several reasons why the military has these different groups available for special missions. US Special Operations Command (SOCOM) makes sure that these groups all work

Army Green Berets run out of a UH-60 Black Hawk helicopter at a US Marine Corps training center.

together and function without overlapping and getting in each other's way.

One way to think about the need for so many Special Operations Forces groups is to compare them to doctors. All doctors go to medical school, and they can generally diagnose and treat many different medical conditions. But most doctors also have a specialty, such as orthopedics, dermatology, or pediatrics. It means that they are experts in that particular specialty. So, when people break bones, they usually go to

THE COAST GUARD

While all other branches of the US military operate under the Department of Defense, the US Coast Guard operates under the Department of Homeland Security. The coast guard does have its own version of a special forces group, but it is not operated under SOCOM. The coast guard's special forces group is called the Deployable Operations Group (DOG). It is a command group that can provide specialized coast guard units to the Department of Defense, the Department of Justice, and other command groups if needed. These specialized units include coastguardsmen who have high-level law enforcement skills or who can respond quickly to catastrophes such as oil spills and hurricanes. These coast guard units can deploy within 24 hours and set up operations wherever they are needed.

an orthopedic surgeon. If they have skin problems, they see a dermatologist. And if the patients are children, their parents take them to a pediatric doctor.

The Special Operations Forces groups of the US military operate in a similar way. While they are all highly trained in most combat tactics and can be used for many special operations, each group specializes in certain types of missions. Rod Powers, a retired air force sergeant, wrote an article about special forces operations, explaining:

> If one wished to attach explosives under the water line on an enemy ship, for example, Army Rangers would not be the best choice. In this instance, the Special Operations Force with the most training and experience in underwater

combat operations would be Navy SEALs. On the other hand, if one needed to deploy a highly trained light infantry force well inland, behind enemy lines, to destroy a significant military target, you can't do much better than a company of Army Rangers.[1]

Each Special Operations Forces group specializes in certain types of missions carried out in certain conditions and using certain equipment and training. The problem with having several specialized groups belonging to different branches of the military, however, was making sure they could work together seamlessly when necessary.

A MISSION THAT WENT WRONG

The need for one overall command system for the Special Operations Forces became apparent when a mission went tragically wrong. In 1980, a group of American hostages was

SOCOM AT A GLANCE

Just what is the specific mission of SOCOM? It trains all Special Operations Forces units and then sends them on missions all over the world. It also makes sure that all Special Operations Forces are working together and with other branches of the military. Special operations missions can include hostage rescue, counterterrorism, eliminating weapons of mass destruction, helping other countries with their own internal conflicts, and providing humanitarian assistance in times of natural disasters or other emergencies.

being held captive in the US Embassy in Tehran, Iran. They were captured in November 1979 when militant Iranian students seized the embassy to protest the fact that the US government was allowing the former leader of Iran to travel to the United States for medical treatment. Some hostages were released, but 52 of them were held in the embassy for 14 months.

US president Jimmy Carter eventually ordered a special military mission, called Operation Eagle Claw, to rescue the hostages. On April 24, 1980, eight helicopters were supposed to begin the attack, but three of them failed before they could even leave the staging area, known as Desert One. The helicopters were critical to the mission, so it had to be cancelled. However, when the helicopters began withdrawing from the area, one of them collided with a transport plane. Eight soldiers were killed, and five were critically injured. The hostages would not be released for another 270 days.[2]

The failed operation highlighted several issues in the US military and its Special Operations Forces units. Funding for these units had been shrinking, and following the Vietnam War, there had been a decline in the number of well-qualified and capable soldiers. This was mostly due to the ending of the draft, which had required male US citizens ages 18 to 25 to register for the military. According to retired Lieutenant General Sam Wilson:

★ The failed Operation Eagle Claw resulted in a helicopter crashing into an airplane, killing eight soldiers.

> *That crushing failure at Desert One and its consequences told everyone, despite the enormous talent we had, we hadn't put it together right and something had to be done. . . . Once again, our service components could not talk with each other, the forces had not lived together, trained together, nor did we share the same doctrine. The operation was like a pick-up basketball game. Desert One [showed] us something must be done.[3]*

After several years of studies into the effectiveness of the special forces and military operations, the Department of Defense created the Joint Special Operations Agency on

OPERATION EAGLE CLAW

The military's detailed plan for rescuing the Tehran hostages relied heavily on many different Special Operations Forces groups working together. Part of the reason for the failure of the mission was lack of communication and the difficulty in coordinating so many different groups over long distances and with a tight timetable. Hearings about the failed mission took place with the Senate Armed Services Committee. The committee asked Delta Force Commander Colonel Charles A. Beckwith what he had learned from the mission failure, and what he would do differently if he could do it again. Beckwith responded:

> If [football] coach Bear Bryant at the University of Alabama put his quarterback in Virginia, his backfield in North Carolina, his offensive line in Georgia and his defense in Texas and then got Delta Airlines to pick them up and fly them to Birmingham on game day, he wouldn't have his winning teams. . . . My recommendation is to put together an organization that would include Delta, the Rangers, the Navy SEALs, Air Force pilots, its own staff, its own support people, its own aircraft and helicopters. Make this organization a permanent military unit. Allocate sufficient funds. And give it sufficient time to recruit, assess, and train its people.[4]

Following these hearings, SOCOM was created.

January 1, 1984. But it still did not have enough authority or funding. In 1987, the US Congress, as part of military reforms, voted to provide funding to establish SOCOM instead.

SOCOM'S ROLE

SOCOM brought all the Special Operations Forces groups together under one overall command. Under SOCOM, all of these units can combine their many different skills into the best, most efficient specialized combat force in the world. It also emphasizes a culture of cooperation that works to accomplish missions as a group with unified leadership—not as separate units from separate branches of the military. SOCOM provides better overall funding for the United States' most highly trained, elite soldiers. It also lets them benefit from the specialties and expertise of each group.

SOCOM consists of several different command groups. There is the US Army Special Operations Command, which includes Special Forces (Green Berets), Rangers, Special Operations Aviators, Civil Affairs Soldiers (who specialize in working with civilians and civil authorities), Psychological Operations Units (which deal with information, intelligence, and military deception), Training Cadre (which manages schools for special forces soldiers), and Sustainment Soldiers (who provide logistical and medical support). The Naval Special Warfare Command oversees the SEALs, SWCC, and Enablers (who provide technical support).

SOCOM also includes the Air Force Special Operations Command, which oversees Special Tactics, Special Operations Aviators, and Support Air Commandos. MARSOC is home to the Critical Skills Operators, Special Operations Officers, Special Operations Capabilities Specialists, and Special Operations

Combat Services Specialists. These groups work as teams in all aspects of large and small missions.

To support the special operations units attached to each branch of the military, there are joint command groups that make sure everyone is working together. The Joint Special Operations Command studies the requirements and techniques needed for special operations. It also plans and conducts exercises and training for special forces members and helps develop tactics. There are also several Special Operations Command units in specific locations, including Africa, Europe, Asia, and the

SOCOM AFTER 9/11

Following the terrorist attacks against the United States on September 11, 2001, President George W. Bush spoke to the nation:

We will direct every resource at our command—every means of diplomacy, every tool of intelligence, every instrument of law enforcement, every financial influence, and every necessary weapon of war—to the destruction and to the defeat of the global terror network. . . . Our response involves far more than instant retaliation and isolated strikes. Americans should not expect one battle, but a lengthy campaign unlike any other we have ever seen. It may include dramatic strikes visible on TV and covert operations secret even in success.[5]

The terrorist attacks made the US military rethink its strategies to focus on combating terrorism all over the world. As a result, SOCOM's special forces units became a key part of the military's antiterrorism efforts.

★ President Donald Trump visited the troops at SOCOM's headquarters, MacDill Air Force Base in Florida.

Pacific region, to monitor troubled areas and provide security and support.

With several different Special Operations Forces groups across all the branches of the military, it might seem overwhelming to decide which one is the best possibility for a career. There are many career opportunities within each group. It is helpful to look at each of the Special Operations Forces individually to see what career options there are and how to get started.

TRAINING FOR THE SEALs

Each of the Special Operations Forces has its own intense, specialized training. This comes after basic military training and training for the specific military branch that holds the special forces group. For example, to be accepted to train as a Navy SEAL, a navy sailor has already gone through regular navy basic training.

Before they can be accepted into SEAL training, candidates must pass a physical fitness test. Only the top-ranking candidates are chosen for training, which has multiple phases and lasts more than a year. It includes PRE-BUDS, a seven- to nine-week-long training that prepares sailors for Basic Underwater Demolition/SEAL training (BUD/S).

There are three phases of BUD/S training: basic conditioning, diving, and land warfare. At the end of BUD/S, there is SEAL Qualification Training, which transitions candidates from a basic level of Naval Special Warfare to the more advanced tactical training that SEALs must have before they are ready to join a platoon. After passing BUD/S, there is usually additional training, such as Parachute Jump School, before each SEAL is assigned to a specific team.

CHAPTER 4

NAVY SEALs

The Navy SEALs are one of the most famous of the Special Operations Forces groups. People often recognize the name of this group because of its appearance in television shows, movies, and in the news after the SEALs have participated in a successful high-profile mission. Like members of other Special Operations Forces groups, SEALs undergo intensive and difficult training and testing. This training gives

Parachuting is one of the many specialized skills of Navy SEALs.

them special capabilities in warfare beyond those of the average soldier or sailor. SEAL missions include direct combat, special reconnaissance, fighting terrorism, and defending US interests within other countries. SEALs need to have strong willpower, as well as the ability to think critically and make solid decisions during stressful situations when there are few options. They must be absolutely dedicated to their training and their fellow SEAL team members.

PREPARING FOR SEAL TRAINING

Because SEAL training, especially the physical aspect, is so difficult and demanding, there are many online resources to help potential SEALs prepare to pass the PST and BUD/S training. There are calculators that will tell a potential SEAL where their PST score ranks among other potential SEALs across the country. There are training guides to help prospective SEALs get physically fit enough for the physical training. There are videos and instructions for swimming correctly and getting the timing needed to pass the swimming portion of the PST. One thing that these preparation and training guides have in common is that they stress the need to start training long before attempting to become a SEAL, because a potential SEAL has to be as fit as possible before the process begins.

BECOMING A SEAL

Navy personnel who want to become SEALs must be in top physical shape. Before training to become a SEAL, candidates must take the SEAL Physical Screening Test (PST), which will determine if they have the physical ability to become a SEAL. They must be able to swim a 500-yard (457 m) breaststroke or sidestroke in less than 12.5 minutes, do at least 42 push-ups in two minutes, do at least 50 sit-ups in two minutes, do at least six pull-ups, and run 1.5 miles (2.4 km) in less than 11 minutes.[1] This run has to be done while wearing boots and long pants. And while these are the minimum numbers needed to pass the test, most good or great candidates will do these tasks much more quickly.

While much of SEAL training is about extreme physical fitness and mental abilities, it is just as important to teach SEAL candidates about what being a SEAL is really like. This includes the specific ways that SEALs conduct themselves and what will be expected of them as they keep training. SEALs go on to learn very specialized skills and find themselves in difficult and dangerous training missions.

After being assigned to a team, graduates usually have to complete more training. For example, those who are assigned to a SEAL Delivery Vehicle (SDV) Team for diving medicine and medical skills duty must take the Special Operations Medical Course. Other types of advanced training include foreign language training and training in tactical communications, which are communications that convey important information about tactics and operations from one command headquarters to another. There is also training in specialties such as sniper, free-fall parachuter, jump master (expert paratroopers who teach

MAKING AN IMPACT

Navy SEALs are well-trained and skillful, like Special Operations Forces members in other branches of the military. The greatest strength of Navy SEALs is their ability to conduct operations from the sea and to return to the sea when their mission is done. They are required to use a combination of specialized training, equipment, and tactics to complete special operations missions around the world, especially when those missions need to be done quickly and stealthily. SEALs need the flexibility to adapt to changing situations.

Navy SEALs sometimes use submarines for SDV operations.

other soldiers how to parachute), and explosive breacher, which means using explosives to open closed or locked doors.

SEAL CAREERS

The reason SEALs stands for "Sea, Air, and Land" is because members of this special operations group may find themselves in any one of these environments, depending on what their mission is. After training, a SEAL may become an SDV operator or be assigned to a SEAL platoon. SDV operators are trained to operate special vehicles to insert SEAL team members into combat zones and then take them out again safely when their mission is over. The special vehicles include modified boats, planes, helicopters, and even submarines. An SDV operator may find himself operating in the air, on land, or at sea. Members of SWCC are the most highly trained boat operators, specializing both in weapons and in safely transporting SEAL teams in especially dangerous situations.

After a trained SEAL has been assigned to a platoon, the SEAL is deployed to an area of operation. This might be an area of ongoing conflict, such as Afghanistan, Iraq, or Syria. From there, SEAL members will go on tours of duty that last from three to five years. They will also have additional training in skills such as diving, warfare in specific types of environments (such as cities or deserts), and fighting in close quarters.

SEALs perform different types of activities as part of their assigned missions, some of which require special training. These activities include carrying out direct assaults on places and targets that might be in isolated areas, destroying enemy weapons, and subduing hostile people. SEALs may sometimes collaborate with other Special Operations Forces groups, such as the Army Rangers, for these types of missions.

Other SEAL skills are used for reconnaissance missions, often to gather intelligence information on enemy territory and positions before a SEAL strike. SEALs can infiltrate behind enemy lines and conduct surveillance by air, sea, and land, sending this information back to their command center to help plan a forthcoming mission. They provide information about where the enemy is, what weapons they have, and how many hostile forces there are. They must be skilled in diving,

WOMEN IN THE SEALs

In 2015, the Department of Defense approved admitting women into the Navy SEALs. Before that, women were not allowed to attempt to become Navy SEALs. Alongside this change, the navy said women who wanted to become SEALs would follow the same requirements as men. Although women make up approximately 18 percent of navy personnel, it wasn't until 2017 that a female navy sailor started the process of becoming a SEAL. She later dropped out during training. Another woman passed the SEALs physical screening as of 2018 but did not continue into the training program. As of 2019, no woman had yet to pass the screening, apply, and train for SEALs membership.[2]

★ Navy SEALs use advanced technology during dive operations and other missions.

parachuting, and landing in remote places so that they can sneak into enemy territory without being detected.

Some SEALs specialize in hostage rescue. If government negotiation efforts fail to secure the release of an American being held hostage, a SEAL team can plan a rescue operation. They must be fast, strong, and stealthy. They might have to use speedboats or helicopters. They may need to go on foot through the jungle at night, wearing night-vision goggles so they can surprise the hostage captors at daylight. The actual rescue might require hand-to-hand combat with terrorists. Skilled SEAL teams can rescue hostages in just minutes.

SEAL teams may also have to engage in unconventional warfare. This is warfare that doesn't necessarily take place on a battlefield or during a combat raid. It includes activities such as psychological warfare, which is the process of using propaganda, intimidation, or threats to reduce the enemy's morale. SEALs who are good at foreign languages and international relations might become friends with local people in a place where war or unrest is happening. By befriending these civilians, SEALs can influence how they feel about the United States. If the local people have a good opinion about the United States, then when regular US military troops follow the SEAL team, those local people will be less resistant to them and will make it easier for those troops to operate.

Navy SEALs save people trapped in dangerous situations, and their secret missions ensure the security of the United States. Other military teams rely on the SEALs. Their training gives SEAL team members a broad range of skills, and SEALs can be flexible and quickly adapt to what needs to be done anywhere in the world, at any time.

TOP FIVE QUESTIONS

★ **DOES A NAVY SAILOR HAVE TO BE AN OFFICER TO BE IN THE SEALs?**

Navy sailors do not need to be officers to join the SEALs. However, SEAL officers must have been navy officers, which requires a college education. Each SEAL platoon has at least two officers.

★ **WHAT SKILLS ARE USEFUL FOR A PERSON INTERESTED IN BECOMING A NAVY SEAL?**

Navy SEALs must be smart, strong leaders who are able to work well on teams. They must also be as physically fit as possible.

★ **WHAT SHOULD STUDENTS STUDY IN HIGH SCHOOL IF THEY WANT TO BECOME A SEAL?**

Joining the SEALs requires a high school diploma, and the applicant has to be between the ages of 17 and 28. People who are interested in joining the navy and starting SEAL training should study foreign languages, as well as algebra, science, and physics.

★ **DO SEALs ALWAYS GO ON OVERSEAS MISSIONS?**

SEALs go on missions all over the world, often in places where there is war or civil unrest. They must be ready to travel anywhere, on short notice, at any time.

★ **WHAT IS FAMILY LIFE LIKE FOR A NAVY SEAL?**

Many SEALs are married and have families. However, SEAL families have to be aware that their loved one may often be on secret missions far away, and they may be unable to communicate at that time. SEAL families are provided with housing and many other support services on the naval bases where they live.

CHAPTER 5

THE GREEN BERETS

The Green Berets are one of the most well-known and respected Special Operations Forces units. Their formal title is the US Army Special Forces, and they are known to be the most versatile and adaptable Special Operations Forces unit in the military. Their motto is "De Oppresso Liber," which is Latin for "To Free the Oppressed."

Green Berets soldiers practice shooting with M4A1 rifles.

BECOMING A GREEN BERET

All US Army soldiers' careers start the same way, regardless of whether they're pursuing a Special Forces job. All people entering the US military must take the Armed Services Vocational Aptitude Battery (ASVAB). Then they all start with basic combat training, often called boot camp. Green Berets begin by enlisting in the US Army and attending boot camp for about ten weeks. This training takes place in three phases: Red, White, and Blue. The Red Phase includes general orientation and a basic introduction to the skills and knowledge required to be a soldier. The White Phase includes fitness training and learning how to handle weapons. The Blue Phase includes advanced marksmanship and maneuvering and ends with a land-navigation challenge that lasts several days. After recruits have passed all of this training, they are given a black army beret to wear. This indicates that they are fully qualified army soldiers.

But for soldiers who want to join the Special Forces unit, basic army training is only the beginning. To be a Green Beret, a soldier must complete Advanced Individual Training and attend the US Army Airborne School. Only after completing these requirements are they eligible for Special Forces training. It starts with the Special Operations Preparation Course (SOPC), a two-week course that is meant to prepare candidates to take the test that will admit

ASVAB TEST

The Armed Services Vocational Aptitude Battery (ASVAB) is a timed aptitude test that is given both at high schools and at military entry processing stations, where soldiers first enlist. The ASVAB is meant to measure four areas: arithmetic reasoning, word knowledge, paragraph comprehension, and mathematics knowledge. The scores count toward the Armed Forces Qualifying Test (AFQT) score. The AFQT score determines whether a person is qualified to enlist in the military. These scores also help determine how qualified a soldier is for certain military specialties and can improve the chances of being accepted for training in those specialties.

them to the Special Forces. The SOPC focuses on physical fitness and land navigation skills, which are extremely important to Special Forces soldiers.

The next step to becoming a Green Beret is to pass the Special Forces Assessment and Selection Course (SFAS). To even get into SFAS, a soldier must pass the army physical fitness test with a minimum score of 260 out of a possible 300. The SFAS tests survival skills and emphasizes intense physical and mental skills, which are needed to be part of the elite Special Forces group. SFAS is also considered to be the first phase of Special Forces training. It is followed by the Special Forces Qualification Course (SFQC), which lasts about 53 weeks.[1] The phases of SFQC include training in small unit tactics, advanced Special Forces tactics, survival skills, languages and cultures, unconventional warfare, escape and

WOMEN IN THE GREEN BERETS

In 2016, the US Army began allowing women to apply for the Green Berets. But until 2018, no woman had made it through the SFAS, which is designed to push soldiers to the brink of mental and physical exhaustion. In 2018, a woman finished the SFAS and was chosen for the SFQC training, which would last for more than a year. Retired Lieutenant General Steve Blum, a former Green Beret, told National Public Radio, "I applaud and celebrate the fact because half of the world that we have to deal with when we're out there, half of the people we have to help, are women. The days of men fighting men without the presence of women is long gone."[2]

evasion skills, and advanced combat survival tactics. Each Green Beret soldier is also trained in a particular specialty, such as medical care, communications, engineering, or weapons. Green Berets are expected to have more initiative, self-reliance, maturity, and resourcefulness than the average army soldier. After five phases of training are completed, soldiers graduate from the program and can officially put on their green berets as Special Forces soldiers.

CAREERS IN THE GREEN BERETS

Green Berets are not all trained in exactly the same skills. Each member has his own military occupational specialty (MOS). Within the Green Berets, members are organized into small teams, called Operational Detachment Alphas (ODA). Each ODA has 12 members who are experts in a particular MOS: two weapons sergeants, two communications sergeants, two medical sergeants, and two engineering sergeants. The team also includes a detachment commander, assistant commander (warrant officer), operations sergeant, and assistant operations sergeant. However, the exact makeup of an ODA might differ depending on the specific mission the group is conducting.

The detachment commander holds the rank of captain and has complete authority and responsibility for all members of

★ Green Berets sometimes use specialized equipment or military vehicles, such as ground mobility vehicles.

the team. He has been trained in skills such as unconventional warfare, which are activities that support rebels or guerrilla fighters who are trying to disrupt or overthrow their government or an occupying government force. His duties include training foreign and American soldiers, managing resources, planning missions, and working with US and foreign government agencies. The detachment commander also must be extremely familiar with each of his team members' MOS skills in order to

55

use them to best advantage when planning missions. These missions may take place in peacetime or during conflicts, and the commander must be able to use his soldiers' assets in the most effective way. He may also have to command battalions of soldiers that are not from the United States. They may be from the country where his ODA is on a mission. In order to become a detachment commander, he must already be an army officer, which requires having a college degree.

Each ODA also includes an assistant detachment commander, sometimes called a warrant officer. Assistant commanders can be enlisted members of the army, rather than officers, which means that they do not have to have a college degree. He is second in command of the ODA and assists the detachment commander.

THE SERGEANTS

The other members of the ODA hold the rank of sergeant and are enlisted soldiers, not officers. They include an operations sergeant and assistant. The operations sergeant is in charge of the entire mission.

There are also two weapons sergeants who are trained to operate and maintain a wide variety of weapons from the United States, as well as weapons from US allies and other countries. Because other countries may use weapons that are different from those used in the United States, the weapons sergeant must understand those weapons so that the ODA can perform its mission better.

There are also two engineering sergeants who specialize in construction as well as demolition. They might need to build buildings, bridges, and fortifications in the field. They can also demolish enemy targets such as fueling facilities, bridges, railroads, and roads. There are two medical sergeants who are trained to be among the best trauma and first responder medical technicians in the world. They also have skills in dentistry, veterinary medicine, and optometry, as well as knowledge of public sanitation and water quality. There are also two communications sergeants who can operate any type of

RANKS

Although every branch of the military has a system of ranks for its members, not every system is exactly the same. Ranks are a system that indicate a soldier's level of expertise, responsibility, and authority. Ranks also help determine a soldier's pay. In the army, there are two sets of ranks: one for officers and another for enlisted soldiers. For officers, ranks start with lieutenant, then move up through captain, major, lieutenant colonel, colonel, brigadier general, major general, lieutenant general, general, to general of the army (usually only used in times of war). For enlisted soldiers, ranks start with private, then move up through specialist, corporal, sergeant, master sergeant, sergeant major, and command sergeant major, to sergeant major of the army. Each move upward in rank also includes higher pay and more responsibility.

Some Green Berets are trained to use military working dogs. The dogs may help clear a room by checking for explosives or other dangers.

communications gear or technology, from encrypted satellite communications to old-fashioned Morse code.

The team also includes two intelligence sergeants who gather and process intelligence information. They use this information to see if there are any weaknesses in their team and to protect the team during its mission. They are also trained in all types of intelligence formats, including photography and other digital media, digital information systems, biometrics, and forensics.

All Green Beret sergeants are enlisted soldiers who belong to either the army or the National Guard. National Guard soldiers are eligible to train for the Green Berets, and if they qualify, they can live in any part of the United States and train with the

MAKING AN IMPACT

The Green Berets have skills and duties beyond those of many other Special Operations Forces groups. They can perform combat tasks and reconnaissance, like most Special Operations Forces units, but they also carry out missions far beyond that. Green Berets with the ability to speak many languages may find themselves advising or protecting foreign leaders. Green Berets might train police or paramilitary groups in other countries or carry out a guerrilla-style raid on a drug overlord's headquarters. They are also trained in disinformation, which is the ability to create and spread false information. While they will always work in the interest of the United States, their work is carried out all over the world and may often be unnoticed. They are often called "America's first line of defense" around the globe.

Special Forces companies that they choose to be assigned to. Each Green Beret soldier's specialty depends on his or her scores on special army aptitude tests. Soldiers can earn college degrees while serving in the army as a way to advance to the officer ranks.

TOP FIVE QUESTIONS

★ **DOES A SOLDIER HAVE TO BE AN OFFICER TO BE IN THE GREEN BERETS?**

No, enlisted soldiers can become Green Berets, but they cannot hold officer ranks in the Green Berets.

★ **WHAT SKILLS ARE USEFUL FOR A PERSON INTERESTED IN BECOMING A GREEN BERET?**

Green Berets must be smart and disciplined. They must work well with others, and they must be physically fit.

★ **WHAT SHOULD A STUDENT STUDY IN HIGH SCHOOL IF HE OR SHE IS INTERESTED IN JOINING THE GREEN BERETS?**

Becoming a Green Beret requires a high school diploma. A high school student should also study hard for the subjects on the ASVAB, such as math and English. It may also be useful for students interested in becoming Green Berets to study foreign languages, as Green Berets frequently work with militaries in other countries.

★ **DO GREEN BERETS ALWAYS GO ON OVERSEAS MISSIONS?**

Green Berets are stationed at bases in the United States and overseas, but since their traditional purpose is to advise and train foreign military forces, and also because they fight terrorism, almost all of their missions take place out of the country.

★ **WHAT IS FAMILY LIFE LIKE FOR GREEN BERETS?**

Many Green Berets have spouses and families. Many of their families are provided with housing on a military base.

CHAPTER 6

THE ARMY RANGERS

US Army Rangers are a direct-action fighting force that specializes in raids and assault missions. Their missions are usually deep in enemy territory, and Rangers have to be flexible in adapting to changing conditions in hostile places. Their missions include special operations raids, operations that require seizing and holding enemy positions such as airfields, and special reconnaissance. All Rangers are members of the

Army Rangers are trained to operate in all kinds of terrain and weather conditions.

75th Ranger Regiment, which has five battalions. Rangers have one of the longest histories of all the Special Operations Forces groups, dating back to colonial times. Rangers are considered to be role models for all other soldiers in terms of their physical condition, their mental abilities, and their sense of right and wrong. They are expected to make sound judgments about people and circumstances. The Army Rangers' creed states, "Recognizing that I volunteered as a Ranger, fully knowing the hazards of my chosen profession, I will always endeavor to uphold the prestige, honor, and high esprit de corps of my Ranger Regiment."[1]

BECOMING A RANGER

Any active duty army soldier can volunteer to become part of the Ranger Regiment, but they have to have some basic qualifications. Rangers must also be physically fit enough to pass the Ranger Fitness Test, which requires a sequence of 58 push-ups, 69 sit-ups, a five-mile (8 km) run in 40 minutes or less, and six pull-ups. They also have to pass a water survival assessment and finish a 12-mile (19 km) march wearing a 35-pound (16 kg) pack and a weapon in less than three hours.[2] They must also work in an army MOS that is used in the Ranger Regiment and qualify for airborne training.

If soldiers have these qualifications, they will begin the Ranger Assessment and Selection Program (RASP). Enlisted soldiers and sergeants attend RASP 1 for eight weeks.

THE RANGER MOTTO

The Rangers' famous motto is "Rangers, lead the way!" The motto came from World War II, when Allied forces were landing on the beaches of Normandy, France. During the landing, Allied forces were trapped by enemy fire in a section of Omaha Beach, one of the main landing points for the Allied armies. According to *Army.com*, "General Norman Cota approached and demanded a group of soldiers to identify their unit. 'Fifth Rangers,' a soldier yelled. After some expletives, Cota replied, 'Rangers! Lead the way!'"[3]

It trains them in the basic skills and tactics that they will need to succeed in the Rangers. Phase 1 of RASP 1 tests potential Rangers in areas such as physical fitness, navigation, and retrieving and stabilizing injured personnel, along with a test of Ranger history. Phase 2 trains Ranger candidates in skills such as combat driving, marksmanship, and explosives. Once they finish RASP 1, soldiers have all the training necessary to join the 75th Ranger Regiment. At graduation, they change from the standard army black beret to the tan beret of a Ranger. Officers then have to attend RASP 2, a three-week course that teaches leadership skills for Ranger officers.

After graduating from RASP, Rangers still have more training to complete. All Rangers must attend Ranger School. This lasts

WOMEN RANGERS

In August 2018, Staff Sergeant Amanda Kelley became the first enlisted woman to pass the difficult Ranger training course. Kelley's experience in Ranger school was the same as any man's, including shaving her head. In an interview with *Army Times*, Kelley talked about her experience:

> I can tell you what it's like as a soldier going through. And honestly, it's the same for male and female. We all go through the same thing at the same time. You look left or right and each one of you is hurting just as bad. And you just pick up your rucksack and keep going. . . . I like challenges. And when I was in [Ranger] school I wasn't worried about making history, I wasn't worried about any of that. I was just worried about getting through this training because I didn't want to fail.[4]

for two months and teaches new Rangers advanced skills in close combat and direct-fire battles. It consists of three phases: Crawl, Walk, and Run. During the Crawl phase, which lasts 20 days, soldiers learn the physical and mental skills they must have to perform missions. The Walk phase lasts 21 days and takes place in the mountains.[5] Rangers learn the skills and tactics needed for military mountaineering. They learn how to participate in missions and battles in a mountain environment. The Run phase tests the Rangers' weapons skills and their ability to function well even under extreme mental and physical stress.

ARMY RANGER CAREERS

A Ranger platoon is made up of soldiers who work in various roles and have different abilities. They all work together to

MAKING AN IMPACT

Every Army Ranger battalion is capable of deploying to any place in the world in just 18 hours.[6] Being highly trained and flexible allows them to be on the front lines of any conflict quickly. Rangers have fought since before the United States was a country and have been a part of every military action and war that the United States has participated in since the 1700s. Today, they conduct missions to support global antiterrorism efforts, continually train for combat, and train the next generation of Rangers to carry on the tradition.

★ Sometimes Army Rangers operate from aircraft.

perform successful missions. A platoon typically has about 30 soldiers, and it includes machine gun squads and sniper teams.[7]

There are several different types of leadership roles in a Ranger platoon. The platoon leader and the platoon sergeant make up the headquarters of a platoon, and they generally stay in a command position rather than on the front lines of a conflict. The platoon leader is responsible for planning patrol routes, assigning the different tasks that need to be done, and overseeing all of the other soldiers under his command. The platoon sergeant is second in command and assists the platoon leader. He also handles requests from squad leaders for ammunition, food, and water, along with training and administrative duties, such as maintaining records.

Each platoon is made up of squads of about seven to nine soldiers, each with different skills. Types of squads include the machine gun squad, mortar squad, and rifle squad. A squad leader commands each squad and is responsible for carrying out the mission of that squad. A squad leader is also responsible for maintaining weapons and equipment. He reports to his superior officers on behalf of the squad. There is also a team leader for each team within a squad.

There are several other roles within each platoon as well. The lead medic has responsibility for all first aid and medical evacuation situations and directs the squad members who carry out these tasks. This person also supervises all the general health and hygiene aspects of the platoon. The radio operator handles all communications with both the platoon squads and the company headquarters. This person is generally located within the headquarters with the platoon leader and platoon sergeant. The forward observer (FO) is basically the eyes and ears of the entire platoon. This person locates targets and directs weapons firing. The FO also knows the terrain the platoon is operating on and the unit's plan for firing and maneuvering.

Each Ranger has a military specialty. These include many different skills, such as weapons, construction, aircraft repair, unmanned vehicle operation, telecommunications intelligence, psychological operations, medicine, transportation, food service, parachute rigging, and many more. These specialties help determine which task each Ranger will be assigned to do, depending on the needs of the mission.

TOP FIVE QUESTIONS

- ★ **DOES A SOLDIER HAVE TO BE AN OFFICER TO BE IN THE RANGERS?**
  Enlisted soldiers may become Rangers; they do not need to be officers. But to be an officer in the Rangers, a soldier must already be an army officer. They also have to undergo additional training to become Ranger officers.

- ★ **WHAT SKILLS ARE USEFUL FOR A PERSON INTERESTED IN BECOMING AN ARMY RANGER?**
  Army Rangers must be physically fit. They must be smart and able to work well with others.

- ★ **WHAT SHOULD STUDENTS STUDY IN HIGH SCHOOL IF THEY WANT TO BE IN THE ARMY RANGERS?**
  Becoming a Ranger requires a high school diploma. High school students should also study for the subjects on the ASVAB, such as math and English, as well as any subject they might like to learn as army soldiers.

- ★ **DO RANGERS ALWAYS GO ON OVERSEAS MISSIONS?**
  Army Rangers go on missions all over the world. They are assigned to army bases, which may be in the United States or overseas, but they can be deployed anywhere.

- ★ **WHAT IS FAMILY LIFE LIKE FOR ARMY RANGERS?**
  Many Rangers are married and have families. There are many special facilities, services, benefits, and activities for Rangers' families.

CHAPTER 7

THE MARINES SPECIAL OPERATIONS FORCES

The two Special Operations Forces groups within the US Marine Corps—Force Recon and MARSOC—are known for their ability to find and infiltrate even the most difficult, hidden places in the world and to rescue hostages from dangerous situations. Force Recon gathers intelligence and provides

Recon marines must work well together to successfully complete their missions.

reconnaissance, which is gathering information for missions. MARSOC is a group of raiders trained in direct-action fighting, special reconnaissance, and unconventional warfare. MARSOC was created in 2006, after the 9/11 attacks prompted heightened awareness of terrorism. MARSOC operates under SOCOM and performs its missions under that command. Force Recon belongs exclusively to the US Marine Corps and is under its control and command, but it can still provide resources to SOCOM operations.

QUALIFICATIONS

To become a MARSOC Marine Raider, a person must first have been in the marine corps for three years. Then they can go through a Phase 1 Assessment and Selection Preparatory and Orientation Course (ASPOC) for three weeks. In this course, MARSOC candidates are challenged physically and mentally to see if they really have what is needed to become a raider. Phase 2 is a three-week process in which MARSOC command leaders decide which candidates have the attributes and personality to be part of the special operations unit.[1]

Successful candidates then take the Marine Special Operations Individual Training Course (ITC), which takes place at the Marine Special Operations School at Camp LeJeune, North Carolina. The nine-month course teaches candidates all

MAKING AN IMPACT

The Marine Special Operations Forces of Force Recon and MARSOC are known for their ability to infiltrate places around the world, no matter how well hidden or protected, to perform reconnaissance or gather information. They are also skilled at combat missions and hostage rescues. Like the Special Operations Forces groups in every branch of the military, Force Recon and MARSOC members have been specially trained to take on delicate, sensitive, difficult, and highly secret missions that cannot be performed by average soldiers.

the skills they will need to be effective special operators.[2] The course consists of four phases: basic skills, small unit tactics, close quarters battle, and irregular warfare. Through these phases, candidates learn skills that include direct-action fighting, close-quarters combat, special forms of reconnaissance, caring for casualties, resisting and escaping from capture, survival skills, and weapons skills. Once they have completed all of the phases successfully, the new raiders will be assigned to one of three Marine Raider battalions within MARSOC. Officer candidates also have to take a four-week Team Commanders Course after they complete the ITC.[3]

In Force Recon training, candidates attend the Basic Reconnaissance Course at the School of Infantry West Reconnaissance Training Company, located in Camp Pendleton, California. The school consists of three phases. During the first phase, the Force Recon candidates spend four weeks training on physical skills such as running, completing obstacle courses, ocean swimming with fins, and rucking (running while carrying a weighted backpack). It also includes training in land navigation, helicopter rope suspension, and communications. In Phase 2, they spend three weeks learning small unit tactics and mission planning, then participate in a nine-day mission exercise. The two weeks of Phase 3 are spent in Coronado, California, where candidates work on amphibious reconnaissance, boat

★ MARSOC raiders prepare a boat called a combat rubber raiding craft during training.

operations, and nautical navigation.[4] Once Force Recon candidates have passed all these phases and become Recon marines, they go on to receive more specific training in skills such as survival, diving, and parachuting, as well as many other specialized skills that relate to the specific jobs they will be doing.

CAREERS IN FORCE RECON AND MARSOC

In MARSOC, there are three career specialties: critical skills operator (CSO), special operations officer (SOO), and special operations capabilities specialists and combat service support (SOCS). A CSO is skilled in all special combat operations including reconnaissance and counterterrorism. CSOs are also experts in specific areas such as communications, engineering, special weapons, intelligence, advanced special operations, and language skills. CSOs can perform many different tasks across multiple specialties. An SOO is an officer who serves in a command role. SOCS members are marines who are experts in areas such as intelligence, controlling and carrying out artillery

COMPETING SPECIAL FORCES?

After SOCOM was formed, the US Marine Corps wanted to keep a special forces group that was only under its command. That is why MARSOC is under SOCOM's command but Force Recon remains only under the marine corps' command. The two groups often compete for the most-qualified marine candidates. Sometimes they compete for missions, too. Some people have suggested that the marines combine the two groups into one, but others say it's useful to have both groups. Marine Lieutenant Colonel Eric Thompson said, "When there's not a big war going on, there's always going to be competition between the services for that juicy mission. But if we do go in to combat or a major war starts up, which happens regularly throughout our history, there's going to be plenty of work for both."[5]

and naval gunfire, communications, and canine operations. SOCS members generally serve one tour of duty with MARSOC.

Force Recon marines use their special skills to accomplish a variety of missions. These may be green operations, which require small units doing long-range, stealthy reconnaissance. Other units may participate in black operations, which involve active combat with an enemy and often require airplane and artillery support groups as well.

TOP FIVE QUESTIONS

★ **DOES A MARINE HAVE TO BE AN OFFICER TO BE IN FORCE RECON OR MARSOC?**

A marine does not have to be an officer to join the Marine Special Operations Forces. However, Marine Special Operations Forces officers must have been regular marine officers first, which requires a college education.

★ **WHAT SKILLS ARE USEFUL FOR A PERSON INTERESTED IN ENTERING MARINE SPECIAL OPERATIONS FORCES?**

People interested in MARSOC and Force Recon should develop leadership skills, learn to be team players, and become as physically fit as possible, especially in swimming.

★ **WHAT SHOULD HIGH SCHOOL STUDENTS INTERESTED IN MARINE SPECIAL OPERATIONS FORCES STUDY?**

Joining the marines requires a high school diploma. Students interested in eventually joining the Marine Special Operations Forces, where they could be deployed in overseas areas and interact with local people, would benefit from studying foreign languages, as well as algebra, science, and physics.

★ **DO MARINE SPECIAL OPERATIONS FORCES ALWAYS GO ON OVERSEAS MISSIONS?**

Marine Special Operations Forces units serve both in the United States and all over the world, going wherever they are needed, often with very little notice. They may often be called to perform missions in parts of the world that are experiencing political unrest or conflict.

★ **WHAT IS FAMILY LIFE LIKE FOR MARINE SPECIAL OPERATIONS FORCES MEMBERS?**

Many Force Recon and MARSOC marines are married and have families. However, their families have to be aware that Special Operations Forces marines may often be on secret missions very far away, and they may not be able to communicate at that time. Marine families are provided with housing and many other support services on the military bases where they live.

CHAPTER 8

AIR FORCE SPECIAL OPS

For Air Force Special Ops, one of the unofficial mottos is "Any place. Any time. Anywhere." They are the most specialized members of the air force, and often the Special Operations Forces units of other military branches ask for help from Air Force Special Ops when their skills and training are needed for a successful mission. Their official motto is "First There," and that is exactly the role of Special Ops airmen: they

Air Force Special Ops crews use different military aircraft, including the HH-60G Pave Hawk helicopter.

are often the first ones to land in a hostile location or combat situation, and they lead the way for other forces. Special Ops airmen set up assault zones or airfields, conduct air traffic control, carry out air strikes, and establish command and control to organize operations in a combat situation. They also provide counterterrorism efforts, humanitarian assistance, and special reconnaissance.

QUALIFICATIONS

Members of the US Air Force who are interested in joining the Special Ops unit have to meet several physical qualifications first. They have to have joined the air force before age 28. They must have excellent eyesight, meet specific height and weight standards, and be able to pass a physical exam. Then they must pass the Physical Ability Stamina Test (PAST), which is designed to assess whether they have the minimum fitness level needed for joining the Special Ops group. The PAST has specific requirements that depend on what position the candidate is seeking in the Special Ops group, but candidates must pass every element of the test. It includes timed underwater and surface swimming with several different swimming strokes, as well as running, pull-ups, sit-ups, and push-ups.

SPECIAL OPS CAREERS

Training for Special Ops depends on which specific career an air force member is pursuing within the Special Ops group. There are four different specialties: combat controller (CCT), an air traffic controller who guides and manages aircraft; pararescue (PJ); special reconnaissance (SR); and tactical air control party (TACP). CCT specialists carry out some of the most difficult missions in the entire military. They go to remote, often hostile areas, usually as an individual specialist attached to another

Special Operations Forces team. They are also trained in scuba diving, parachuting, and even snowmobiling. CCTs are also air traffic controllers certified by the Federal Aviation Administration (FAA). They are first on hand to set up air traffic operations and control.

Pararescue airmen are trained to rescue injured airmen, often from hard-to-reach or hostile areas, and bring them home. PJs rescue military personnel all over the world and treat them for injuries. They receive training as parachutists, scuba divers, and rock climbers. They even train in harsh climates such as the Arctic in case they are called to a similar environment to perform a rescue.

The special reconnaissance specialty is responsible for providing the information and battlefield awareness needed for any mission. SR specialists can deploy in any way they need

MAKING AN IMPACT

Members of any of the Air Force Special Ops specialties can have a huge impact, especially because of their skills in preparing battle areas, rescuing injured personnel, and handling air traffic and air strikes. They often work with other branches of the military because of their very specialized skills. This means that they may be saving the lives of many troops, either by directly rescuing them or by battle planning. They go wherever they are needed and support any other military unit.

81

to—by land, sea, or air—to go behind enemy lines and collect information that is needed to prepare for combat. They can use their information to develop a plan based on the enemy's weaknesses or vulnerabilities and to find targets. These actions can change the outcome of any hostilities in the military's favor. They use the latest technology to make sure the military groups that rely on them will have superior access to space, air, and cyberspace from anywhere in the world.

OTHER SPECIALISTS

Air Force Special Ops groups may also include two other specialties that are not strictly part of the Special Operations Forces but often work alongside them. The first is combat weathermen, who work in areas of conflict and track the weather to anticipate ways that battle planning might be affected by weather. This information helps commanders decide how to operate. There are also survival, evasion, resistance, and escape (SERE) specialists, who are experts at techniques such as building shelters, finding water, evading enemies, and navigation. They train other Special Ops personnel to help keep their own unit's members alive and healthy until they can be rescued.

The tactical air control party (TACP) airmen specialize in air strikes, or attacks made by aircraft. They are usually on the front lines, working alongside army and marine units, and they can call down an air strike on any target at an exact time. They are highly trained in physical, mental, and technical areas so that they

★ An Air Force Special Ops recruiter prepares a truck and trailer for a trip to recruit more airmen for Special Ops.

Air Force Special Ops training includes obstacle courses among many other ★ challenges to test candidates' physical fitness and teamwork.

can deal with the harsh conditions of a battle and provide the necessary firepower.

TRAINING FOR AIR FORCE SPECIAL OPS

Candidates for all four Special Ops specialist categories receive the same basic military training course, which lasts for eight weeks.[1] This course teaches candidates about the structure of the military and the core values of the air force, and it prepares them for life as a member of the air force. Basic training is followed by the Special Warfare Preparatory Course (SW PREP), which works on building strength and conditioning through running, swimming, and rucking. After this course, airmen take the PAST test to see if they are fit to proceed to Special Ops training.

Once these steps have been successfully completed, candidates must go through an assessment for the specialty they want to join to see if they are a good fit. Once they have been accepted, the training for each of the four specialties becomes more specific. CCT operators go through a Special Warfare Pre-Dive Course, which lasts four weeks and teaches water skills and confidence as well as preparing them for the Special Warfare Combat Dive Course. That course lasts five weeks and teaches them how to be expert divers. Then the

SPECIAL OPS WOMEN

According to research from the Center for a New American Security, women in the air force have had the most success in the Special Ops specialties, compared with women in the Special Operations Forces of other branches of the military:

> *The Air Force Special Operations Command (AFSOC) has had the most success in integrating women as leaders throughout their [Special Operations Forces] ranks. . . . For example, Lieutenant Colonel Allison Black is nicknamed the "Angel of Death" for her skills while flying an AC-130 gunship into Northern Afghanistan's insurgent territory in 2001. She provided critical cover and fire to the US special operations teams and Afghanistan's Northern Alliance fighters on the ground. Additionally, she has gone on to serve in many leadership roles across AFSOC, including as the 319th Special Operations Squadron commander.*[3]

CCT airmen attend a three-week Airborne School to learn parachuting, a three-week Military Freefall Course to learn skydiving, and a survival, evasion, resistance, and escape (SERE) course to teach them how to survive in hostile climates and locations. Then they take an 11-week course in air traffic control and earn their FAA certification. After that, they spend eight weeks in a Combat Control Apprentice Course to learn air traffic control in battlefield situations. Finally, they spend six months in Special Tactics Training to learn about weapons, demolition, and vehicle operation.[2] After all of that training, they become fully qualified CCTs.

Pararescue airmen also attend the Special Warfare Pre-Dive Course, the Special Warfare Combat Dive Course, the Airborne School, the Military Freefall Course, and SERE training. Then they take the seven-week Pararescue EMT-B Course to train in basic emergency medicine, followed by 30 weeks of the Pararescue EMT-P Course, in which they continue their medical training and become certified paramedics. Their training finishes with 22 weeks of the Pararescue Apprentice Course, where they learn how to apply their medical training in the stress of battlefield conditions.[4]

Special reconnaissance candidates follow the same training schedule up through the SERE training. Then they begin their specialized training with an eight-week Special Reconnaissance Course, which combines fitness training with learning how to collect any data that might be necessary in a battle situation. This is followed by the eight-week Special Reconnaissance Apprentice Course, where they learn weapons and tactics skills as well as how to apply their training to battle situations. Finally, they take six months of Special Tactics Training in advanced weapons, demolition, and special vehicle operation.[5]

TACP candidates have a slightly different training path. They also take the basic training, but then they move on to a TACP Preparatory Course for one week, where they get extreme physical training. Then they take the 12-week TACP Apprentice

Course, where they learn radio communication, small unit tactics, and the basics of air support.[6] After that, they attend Airborne School and SERE training, which completes their training as TACP specialists.

TOP FIVE QUESTIONS

★ **DO AIR FORCE MEMBERS NEED TO BE OFFICERS TO BE IN AIR FORCE SPECIAL OPS?**

A member of the air force does not have to be an officer to join the Special Ops. However, only air force officers can become Special Ops officers.

★ **WHAT SKILLS ARE USEFUL FOR A PERSON INTERESTED IN JOINING AIR FORCE SPECIAL OPS?**

People interested in Air Force Special Ops should develop leadership skills, learn to be team players, and be as physically fit as possible. Experience in flying or skydiving can also be helpful.

★ **WHAT SHOULD A STUDENT STUDY IN HIGH SCHOOL IF HE OR SHE WANTS TO BE IN THE AIR FORCE SPECIAL OPS?**

Joining the air force requires a high school diploma. Students who are interested in joining Special Ops should study algebra, science, and physics, as well as courses related to medicine if they want to be in pararescue.

★ **DO AIR FORCE SPECIAL OPS MEMBERS ALWAYS GO ON OVERSEAS MISSIONS?**

Air Force Special Ops units sometimes serve in the United States, but they may go all over the world, traveling where they are needed. They may often be called to perform missions in parts of the world that are experiencing political unrest or conflict, and they are called to be the first ones on the ground in dangerous situations.

★ **WHAT IS FAMILY LIFE LIKE FOR AIR FORCE SPECIAL OPS MEMBERS?**

Many Air Force Special Ops members are married and have families. However, their families have to know what it means for a spouse or parent to be part of the Special Ops. It means limited ability to communicate and being far away from home frequently. Families are given housing on Air Force bases and have access to services such as health care, schools, and stores.

CHAPTER 9

THE BEST OF THE BEST OF THE BEST

Every Special Operations Forces group within each branch of the military is made up of members who are the best of their particular branch. They have trained harder, learned more, and pushed themselves far beyond the usual limits. But within

Some members of Delta Force are recruited from the Green Berets.

these already selective groups, there are two that are even more specialized: Delta Force and SEAL Team 6.

DELTA FORCE

Delta Force, which is part of the US Army, is perhaps better known than most special forces groups because it is frequently featured in movies and television shows. Delta Force is a group created entirely to combat terrorism around the world. It is a Tier 1 military group, which means members are trusted to carry out the most difficult and delicate missions. These missions include capturing or killing people who are considered to be high value units (HVUs). Those people are of high importance because they are terrorists or people who are vital to an enemy commander in order to carry out a terrorist or enemy mission. Examples of HVUs in recent actions include Osama bin Laden and members of the al-Qaeda terrorist group, which was responsible for the 9/11 attack against the United States. Delta Force is unusual in that its commanders and members keep a very low profile, remaining even more secretive than other members of Special Operations Forces.

JOINING DELTA FORCE

Because Delta Force is extremely elite and secretive, the process for becoming an operator in this group is more complicated than for the other special forces groups. Most Delta Force operators are recruited from the Army Rangers and the Green Berets. However, Delta Force will accept applicants from any part of the military, including the National Guard. Because Delta Force operators have to perform many unusual and secretive missions, they must be evaluated individually, rather than meeting one standard set of qualifications.

Delta Force runs selections for new operators twice a year in a mountainous area of the eastern United States. Selection lasts for three to four weeks and consists of many grueling

★ Delta Force is based in Fort Bragg, North Carolina, where the Army Special Operations headquarters is located.

exercises that evaluate a candidate's physical fitness, stamina, and determination.[1] Candidates are tested on their land navigation skills using maps and compasses, as well as a series of marches and runs over long distances and difficult terrain while carrying heavy loads in their rucksacks. Once they pass the physical tests, operator candidates then go through a series of mental and psychological tests. Candidates who successfully pass those tests are accepted into the Operator Training Course (OTC), which lasts for six months.[2] Once they have completed OTC, the recruits are full operators and join one of the Delta Force squadrons.

The roles, missions, and specific training of Delta Force are secretive, as is most of the information about the group. As one of the most elite Special Operations Forces groups, Delta Force operatives do not have specific careers or jobs. Instead, they have extensive training in many different areas. Operators may specialize in certain skills, but overall, every operator is able to function in any mission. They do hold ranks like the rest of the US military, and there are officers who command each squadron.

SEAL TEAM 6

There is another Special Operations Forces group as elite and secretive as Delta Force. SEAL Team 6—or by its newer official name, US Naval Special Warfare Development Group (DEVGRU)—was created in 1980 when the US Navy realized it needed its own elite counterterrorism team, highly skilled in rescues and missions at sea. While SEAL Team 6 was originally created for maritime special operations, its training has now grown to the point where its members are able to operate anywhere, under any circumstances. Like Delta Force, its primary function is counterterrorism, and its operations are very secretive. But SEAL Team 6 is famous for high-risk hostage and personnel rescues, actions against terrorists and pirates, and working with government agencies such as the CIA.

JOINING SEAL TEAM 6

SEAL Team 6 recruits only from navy personnel who are already Navy SEALs. If someone who is already a SEAL applies for SEAL Team 6 but does not meet the qualifications, they still remain a member of the SEALs. The process for joining SEAL

MAKING AN IMPACT

The impact of SEAL Team 6 and Delta Force will never be clearly known because their members operate in secrecy. Some of their activities appear in the news: hostage rescues, the killing or capture of terrorists and high-value targets, anti-piracy situations, and the protection of important Americans. But much of what they do will never be known to most American citizens.

★ Navy SEALs may eventually go on to apply for SEAL Team 6.

Team 6 can last from months to years, depending on the needs of the group at that time.

Once a SEAL is accepted into SEAL Team 6, he begins training, which is called Green Team. Green Team training is a more intense, specialized version of SEAL training. It consists of three phases. The first phase is close quarters battle (CQB) training. This training develops skills in high-pressure scenarios that involve shooting in small, often enclosed places, usually inside buildings. Trainees have to enter a building and clear it of enemies. While most SEALs have already been through some CQB training, it is more difficult in Green Team training, with more complicated scenarios that the trainees must be able to react to in just seconds. There may be unexpected elements, such as opening a door in order to evacuate a room and finding a brick wall there instead.

The next phase is training in parachuting techniques. Recruits also practice jumping in formation, which is called stacking, as well as skydiving at night. This is followed by SERE training, which trains candidates to survive where there are few resources such as food or shelter, to keep from being captured, and to stay hidden and avoid being discovered by an enemy. SEAL Team 6 candidates also train in hand-to-hand combat, driving military vehicles in battle, mountain climbing, advanced

HEROES OR KILLERS?

In 2015, the *New York Times* published an article about the history of SEAL Team 6 and its quiet operations that included spying on, capturing, and killing enemies. The article drew thousands of reactions from readers. Some thanked SEAL Team 6 for its activities, while others condemned the group for its harsh tactics. One reader said, "I'm very glad we have men like those in Seal Team 6 who are trained to perform with complete efficiency in desperately difficult situations." But other readers spoke against the violent tactics SEAL Team 6 has used, such as a reader who said, "These are trained murderers who serve a very dark and disturbing agenda of the establishment." A comment from a father from Florida summed up his feelings in support of SEAL Team 6:

> *Did anyone even consider who these men really are? They are husbands, sons, fathers, brothers, uncles. They are college graduates, Eagle Scouts, captain of their sports team. They put their life on the line every single day for you and me, protecting our freedom. Have you done that? If you haven't, then don't question something you know nothing about. My son lies in Arlington [National Cemetery] next to his brave teammates of Extortion 17 [whose helicopter was shot down in Afghanistan, killing 17 SEALs]. Don't ever forget their sacrifices.*[3]

97

diving techniques, battle communication, operating in cold weather, and attacking enemy ships.

Once SEAL Team 6 recruits make it through training, they are assigned to one of the SEAL Team 6 squadrons. There are six squadrons, each named by a specific color: Red, Gold, Blue, Silver, Black, and Gray. Each squadron has its own insignia and unique specialty and is divided into several teams. Specialties might include reconnaissance, acting as bodyguards (called close protection), sniping, and gathering intelligence. Specific squadrons are sent around the world to carry out extremely secretive SEAL Team 6 missions.

MANY GROUPS, ONE PURPOSE

As a whole, all of the Special Operations Forces groups from across the US military exist to protect the United States and its citizens. Some are very visible and often appear in the news and popular media, while others will only be guessed at from rumors and work in great secrecy. But the men and women who join these special operations units share one thing: a commitment to serve their country.

TOP FIVE QUESTIONS

★ **DO MILITARY MEMBERS NEED TO BE OFFICERS TO BE IN DELTA FORCE?**

It is not necessary to be an officer to join Delta Force. Officers who do join will also be officers within Delta Force. They must pass the same training requirements as enlisted men.

★ **WHAT SKILLS ARE USEFUL FOR A PERSON INTERESTED IN DELTA FORCE OR SEAL TEAM 6?**

Both of these special operations groups demand extreme fitness and the ability to learn complicated skills. Strong leadership skills and teamwork are important. Experience in skydiving, piloting an aircraft, or scuba diving is also helpful.

★ **WHAT SHOULD A STUDENT STUDY IN HIGH SCHOOL IF HE OR SHE WANTS TO BE PART OF EITHER DELTA FORCE OR SEAL TEAM 6?**

Students interested in either of these groups should study physics, foreign languages, history, and math, especially algebra and geometry.

★ **DO SEAL TEAM 6 AND DELTA FORCE MEMBERS ONLY GO ON DANGEROUS MISSIONS?**

These two groups are very elite and highly trained, so they will be sent on the most dangerous, difficult, and sensitive missions.

★ **WHAT IS FAMILY LIFE LIKE FOR DELTA FORCE AND SEAL TEAM 6 MEMBERS?**

Delta Force and SEAL Team 6 members can have families. These family members understand that Delta Force and SEAL Team 6 members may not be able to communicate easily or at all at times, and may be sent to secret locations that are far away. Family members may not know exactly where their soldier is or what he or she is doing.

ESSENTIAL FACTS

US SPECIAL OPERATIONS FORCES HISTORY

★ 1700s: The Army Rangers are founded before the United States is even a country.
★ 1943: The Navy SEALS are formed from the Naval Construction Battalions (known as the Seabees).
★ 1952: The Army Green Berets, which were originally part of the Office of Strategic Services (OSS), become their own official group.
★ 1977: The Army Delta Force is created.
★ 1980: The Navy's DEVGRU/SEAL Team 6 is formed.
★ 2006: Marine MARSOC is formed following the 9/11 terrorist attacks in 2001.

US SPECIAL OPERATIONS FORCES ORGANIZATION

Each Special Operations Forces group is organized in the same structure as its parent branch of the military. Units, squadrons, groups, and command and rank structures differ according to branch. Special Operations Forces officers have received college educations and became officers prior to joining their special forces branch. Enlisted personnel can become officers or advance through the enlisted ranks of their branch.

CAREER MOVES

How can you prepare for a career in a Special Operations Forces unit?
★ Take high school courses in math, science, and foreign languages.
★ Become very physically fit.
★ Explore the website of the military branch you are interested in to understand requirements and available job specialties.

★ Explore options for receiving college tuition in the military, and decide whether to pursue becoming an officer by attending college before joining.
★ Talk to someone who has been in a Special Operations Forces unit about their experiences.
★ Ask a military recruiter about the best plan for becoming part of a Special Operations Forces group.

IMPACT ON SOCIETY

The Special Operations Forces of the US military are tasked with the most dangerous missions to protect the United States and its interests. Special Operations Forces members are the most highly trained and elite members of the military because they must be able to operate quickly in any type of situation, maintain secrecy, and function well in any type of place or situation. Special Operations Forces members learn teamwork, leadership, problem-solving, and advanced technical skills. These skills can enable them to have well-paying careers in other fields once they leave the military. Above all, they contribute valuable services for protecting their country, even if much of what they do will never be publicly known.

QUOTE

"[After joining Special Ops] I knew that I'd chosen something special, something that was going to make a direct impact on our nation. And I knew I was going to help people on a daily basis."

—*Air Force Master Sergeant Jose Cervantes*

GLOSSARY

amphibious
Working in both land and water.

beret
A type of hat that is round and flat, made of cloth.

biometrics
The measurement and analysis of unique physical attributes like fingerprints or voice patterns.

civilian
A person not serving in the armed forces.

counterterrorism
Strategies to prevent terrorism.

creed
A set of beliefs that guide someone's actions.

deploy
To spread out strategically; to send into battle.

drone
An unmanned aircraft that is basically a flying robot.

embassy
The official place in a foreign country where an ambassador works to represent his or her country.

encrypt
To convert information into a cipher or code to prevent unauthorized access.

forensics
The study of physical evidence such as bloodstains, fingerprints, threads, and hair that helps investigators solve a crime.

guerrilla
A fighter who uses irregular methods, such as sabotage or surprise raids, against a larger force.

intelligence
Information that is of military or political value.

medic
Someone in the military service whose job is to give first aid at combat sites.

mortar
A front-loaded cannon used to fire shells in a high arc.

pararescue
A search-and-rescue mission conducted by people who are trained to parachute into remote or dangerous locations.

platoon
A group of soldiers commanded by a lieutenant and divided into several sections.

rank
An individual's position in military hierarchy.

reconnaissance
An exploration of an area to gather information about the activity of military forces.

unconventional warfare
Military operations that rely on tactics like sabotage, subversion, guerrilla warfare, and gathering intelligence.

ADDITIONAL RESOURCES

Selected Bibliography

Alexander, Nicole, and Lyla Kohistany. "Dispelling the Myth of Women in Special Operations." *Center for a New American Security*, 19 Mar. 2019, cnas.org. Accessed 7 Feb. 2020.

"Explore Careers: Special Forces." *Today's Military*, n.d. todaysmilitary.com. Accessed 7 Feb. 2020.

"US Army Rangers: History & Heritage." *US Army*, n.d. army.mil. Accessed 7 Feb. 2020.

Further Reading

Henzel, Cynthia Kennedy. *US Army*. Abdo, 2021.

Lynch, Chris. *Unconventional Warfare*. Scholastic, 2018.

Webb, Brandon, and Thea Feldman. *Navy SEALs: Mission at the Caves*. Henry Holt, 2018.

Online Resources

To learn more about the US Special Operations Forces, please visit **abdobooklinks.com** or scan this QR code. These links are routinely monitored and updated to provide the most current information available.

More Information

For more information on this subject, contact or visit the following organizations:

John F. Kennedy Special Warfare Museum
Building D-2815, Ardennes and Zabitosky Roads
Fort Bragg, NC 28307
910-432-4272
specialwarfaremuseum.org

This museum, located at the US Army John F. Kennedy Special Warfare Center and School in Fort Bragg, is focused on the history of the army's Special Forces.

Navy SEAL Museum
3300 N. Hwy. A1A
North Hutchinson Island
Fort Pierce, FL 34949
772-595-5845
navysealmuseum.org

This museum has exhibits that focus on the history of the Navy SEALs. It also has a memorial to honor SEALs who died while serving their country.

US Army Airborne & Special Operations Museum
100 Bragg Blvd.
Fayetteville, NC 28301
910-643-2778
asomf.org

This museum focuses on the history of US Army airborne and special operations soldiers from 1940 to the present.

105

SOURCE NOTES

CHAPTER 1. ON THE JOB

1. "Jose Cervantes." *Today's Military*, 2020, todaysmilitary.com. Accessed 12 Sept. 2019.

2. Barbara Starr. "Behind the Scenes with the Commander of Special Ops." *CNN*, 5 Oct. 2015, cnn.com. Accessed 28 Jan. 2020.

CHAPTER 2. A PROUD TRADITION

1. Josh Clark. "How the Green Berets Work." *How Stuff Works*, 2020, science.howstuffworks.com. Accessed 5 Oct. 2019.

2. "September 11 Attacks." *Encyclopedia Britannica*, 26 Nov. 2019, britannica.com. Accessed 28 Jan. 2020.

3. "Defense Primer: Military Enlisted Personnel." *Congressional Research Service*, 16 Dec. 2019, fas.org. Accessed 28 Jan. 2020.

CHAPTER 3. SPECIAL FORCES COMMAND

1. Rod Powers. "US Military Special Operations Forces." *The Balance Careers*, 2 Feb. 2019, thebalancecareers.com. Accessed 28 Jan. 2020.

2. "Iran Hostage Rescue Mission Ends in Disaster." *History*, 28 July 2019, history.com. Accessed 28 Jan. 2020.

3. Alex Hollings. "The Birth of SOCOM: How America's Special Operations Command Was Born of Tragedy." *SOFREP*, 2 Apr. 2019, sofrep.com. Accessed 28 Jan. 2020.

4. Steve Balestrieri. "Operation Eagle Claw, Disaster at Desert One Brings Changes to Special Operations." *SOFREP*, 24 Apr. 2017, sofrep.com. Accessed 6 Oct. 2019.

5. "Text: President Bush Addresses the Nation." *Washington Post*, 20 Sept. 2001, washingtonpost.com. Accessed 28 Jan. 2020.

CHAPTER 4. NAVY SEALS

1. "Navy SEAL Training." *Military*, 2020, military.com. Accessed 14 Oct. 2019.

2. Mark D. Faram. "Two Women Could Enter Navy Special Operations Training This Year." *Navy Times*, 16 Feb. 2018, navytimes.com. Accessed 28 Jan. 2020.

CHAPTER 5. THE GREEN BERETS

1. "Special Forces: Training." *US Army*, 9 Dec. 2019, goarmy.com. Accessed 7 Oct. 2019.

2. Vanessa Romo. "Woman Qualifies for Special Forces Training, Could Be the First Female Green Beret." *National Public Radio*, 16 Nov. 2018, npr.org. Accessed 28 Jan. 2020.

CHAPTER 6. THE ARMY RANGERS

1. "Specialized Ranger Missions." *US Army*, 7 Jan. 2020, goarmy.com. Accessed 9 Oct. 2019.

2. "Specialized Ranger Missions."

3. "Squad Roles." *US Army*, 7 Jan. 2020, goarmy.com. Accessed 10 Oct. 2019.

4. Ron Barnett. "1st Female Enlisted Soldier to Be an Army Ranger Shares Her Story: 'Failure's Not an Option.'" *Army Times*, 2 Nov. 2018, armytimes.com. Accessed 28 Jan. 2020.

5. "Lifestyles." *US Army*, 12 Oct. 2018, goarmy.com. Accessed 9 Oct. 2019.

6. "The Army Rangers: Missions and History." *Military*, 2020, military.com. Accessed 10 Oct. 2019.

7. "Squad Roles."

SOURCE NOTES CONTINUED

CHAPTER 7. THE MARINES SPECIAL OPERATIONS FORCES

1. "Marine Corps Special Forces (MARSOC) Training." *Military*, 2020, military.com. Accessed 15 Oct. 2019.

2. "Marine Corps Special Forces (MARSOC) Training."

3. "Marine Corps Special Forces (MARSOC) Training."

4. "Force RECON Training." *Military*, 2020, military.com. Accessed 15 Oct. 2019.

5. Hope Hodge Seck. "MARSOC and Recon: Does the Corps Need Both?" *Military Times*, 4 Feb. 2014, militarytimes.com. Accessed 28 Jan. 2020.

CHAPTER 8. AIR FORCE SPECIAL OPS

1. "Combat Control." *US Air Force*, n.d., airforce.com. Accessed 16 Oct. 2019.

2. "Combat Control."

3. Nicole Alexander and Lyla Kohistany. "Dispelling the Myth of Women in Special Operations." *Center for a New American Security*, 19 Mar. 2019, cnas.org. Accessed 28 Jan. 2020.

4. "Pararescue." *US Air Force*, n.d., airforce.com. Accessed 16 Oct. 2019.

5. "Special Reconnaissance." *US Air Force*, n.d., airforce.com. Accessed 16 Oct. 2019.

6. "Tactical Air Control Party Specialist (TACP)." *US Air Force*, n.d., airforce.com. Accessed 16 Oct. 2019.

CHAPTER 9. THE BEST OF THE BEST OF THE BEST

1. "Delta Force Selection." *American Special Ops*, 2020, americanspecialops.com. Accessed 19 Oct. 2019.
2. "Delta Force Selection."
3. Nancy Wartik. "Heroes or Killers? A Secret History of SEAL Team 6 Draws a Range of Reader Reaction." *New York Times*, 11 June 2015, nytimes.com. Accessed 28 Jan. 2020.

INDEX

air strikes, 79, 81–82
air traffic control, 25, 79–81, 86
aircrafts, 12, 18, 24, 27, 34, 68, 80, 82, 99
al-Qaeda, 19, 92
Armed Services Vocational Aptitude Battery (ASVAB), 51–52, 61, 69

basic training, 39, 51–52, 85, 87
bin Laden, Osama, 19, 92
boats, 20–21, 23–24, 45, 48, 73
boot camp, 51
Bush, George W., 36

Carter, Jimmy, 32
Central Intelligence Agency (CIA), 16, 18, 95
clinic, 4–6
college education, 23, 49, 56, 60, 77, 97
combat controller (CCT), 25, 80–81, 85–86
commanders, 8, 15, 34, 54–56, 73, 82, 86, 92
communications, 23–24, 43, 54, 59, 68, 73–76, 88, 98
Continental Army, 15
counterterrorism, 10, 18, 22–23, 31, 75, 79, 95
critical skills operator (CSO), 35, 75

Delta Force, 12, 18, 34, 91–92, 94–95, 99
Department of Defense, 12, 22, 30, 33, 46
Desert One, 32–33
DEVGRU/SEAL Team 6, 12, 19, 22, 91, 94–99
dive courses, 85–87
drones, 12, 27
drugs, 5, 10, 59

enemies, 9, 16, 19–20, 25, 30–31, 46–48, 57, 62, 64, 76, 82, 92, 96–98
engineering, 54, 57, 75
enlisted personnel, 10–12, 23–24, 56–57, 59, 61, 64–65, 69, 99
evasion skills, 53, 82, 86, 97
explosives, 5, 30, 45, 65

Federal Aviation Administration (FAA), 81, 86
fitness, 12, 39, 42, 52–53, 64–65, 80, 87, 94, 99
front lines, 8, 25, 66–67, 82

Green Berets, 4, 7, 11, 16–18, 35, 50–54, 59–61, 92
guerrilla warfare, 9, 20, 55, 59

hand-to-hand combat, 48, 97
helicopters, 12, 32, 34, 45, 48, 73, 97
high school, 10, 49, 52, 61, 69, 77, 89, 99
high value units (HVUs), 92
hostages, 10, 31–32, 34, 47–48, 70, 72, 95
humanitarian assistance, 31, 79

injuries, 4, 6, 25, 32, 65, 81
intelligence operations, 8, 22–24, 35–36, 46, 59, 68, 70, 75–76, 98
Iran, 32

kite balloons, 24–25

languages, 12, 43, 48–49, 53, 59, 61, 75, 77, 99
leadership, 35, 65, 67, 77, 86, 89, 99

Marine Special Operations Individual Training Course (ITC), 72–73
medical care, 4–8, 10, 12, 27, 29, 32, 35, 43, 54, 57, 68, 87, 89
mottos, 19, 22, 50, 64, 78

National Guard, 59, 92
navigation, 52–53, 65, 73–74, 82, 94
Navy Combat Demolition Units (NCDUs), 20
Night Stalkers, 11, 18–19

Office of Strategic Services (OSS), 16–17
officers, 23–24, 35, 49, 54, 56–57, 60–61, 65, 68–69, 73, 75, 77, 89, 94, 99
Operation Eagle Claw, 32, 34
operators, 35, 45, 68, 73, 75, 85, 92, 94

110

parachuting, 10, 12, 18, 21, 24, 39, 43, 45, 47, 69, 74, 81, 86, 97
pararescuemen, 10, 25, 80–81, 87, 89
Physical Ability Stamina Test (PAST), 80, 85
physical screening test (PST), 42
piracy, 20, 24, 95
platoons, 39, 45, 49, 66–68
psychological warfare, 35, 48, 69

raids, 9, 19, 23, 48, 59, 62, 71–73
Ranger Assessment and Selection Program (RASP), 64–65
Ranger School, 65
Rangers, 11, 16, 23, 30–31, 34–35, 46, 62–69, 92
ranks, 18, 23, 39, 42, 54–57, 60–61, 86, 94
reconnaissance, 9, 22–25, 41, 46, 59, 62, 71–76, 79–81, 87, 98
running, 42, 64, 66, 73, 80, 85, 94

scuba diving, 24, 81, 99
SEAL Delivery Vehicle (SDV), 43, 45
SEAL Teams, 10–11, 20–21, 31, 34–35, 39–43, 45–49
Second Continental Congress, 15, 19–20
September 11, 2001 terrorist attacks, 19, 36
Signal Corps, 24–25
small unit tactics, 53, 73–74, 76, 88
sniping, 43, 67, 98
Special Forces Assessment and Selection Course (SFAS), 53
special operations capabilities and combat service support (SOCS), 75–76
special operations officer (SOO), 35, 75
Special Tactics Teams, 10, 12, 24–25, 27, 35, 86–87
Special Warfare Combatant-Craft Crewmen (SWCC), 11, 20–21, 35, 45
stamina, 80, 94
submarines, 45
surveillance, 22, 25, 46

Survival, Evasion, Resistance, and Escape (SERE) training, 82, 86–88, 97
survival skills, 12, 53–54, 64, 73–74, 82, 86, 97
swimming, 12, 23, 42, 73, 77, 80, 85

tactical air control party (TACP), 80, 82, 87–88
technology, 12, 59, 82
tests, 13, 39, 40–42, 52–53, 60, 64–66, 80, 85, 94

US Marine Corps, 22, 70–73, 75
US Marine Corps Force Reconnaissance (Force Recon), 11, 24, 70–77
US Marine Corps Forces Special Operations Command (MARSOC), 11, 23–24, 35, 70–73, 75–77
US Special Operations Command (SOCOM), 12, 28, 30–31, 34–36, 71, 75

Vietnam War, 21, 32

Washington, George, 15
weapons, 8, 12, 27, 31, 36, 45–46, 52, 54, 56–57, 64, 66, 68, 73, 75, 86–87
women in the military, 8, 12, 46, 53, 65, 86, 98
World War II, 8, 16–17, 21, 24–25, 64

ABOUT THE AUTHOR

Marcia Amidon Lusted

Marcia Amidon Lusted is the author of 175 books and more than 600 magazine articles for young readers. She also writes and edits for adults.